This book belongs to:

_____→

Dedicated to Shy for helping me with the idea and to all the other superhero military brats out there- my own included.

-Heather

Superheroes' Kids
When Dad is Deployed

By Heather Carson

Illustrated by Angelica Jacquez

Hi friend! My name is Piper

and I know a thing or two.

I've heard that you've been kind of down.

Well, I used to feel just like you.

My daddy goes away like yours does

whether deployed or somewhere training.

All those mixed up emotions we feel

can be just downright draining.

I get sad when my dad isn't here
to tuck me into bed.

I get confused when he says he wishes he was home
but he is somewhere else instead.

I get mad when I can't call him

to tell him about my day.

I get worried he won't remember me,

or that he will always be away.

We know our dads are superheroes

and their jobs sure are rough.

Well, I'll tell you that being a superhero's kid

can sometimes be just as tough.

There is a super secret I can tell you though

that stops me from feeling blue.

Pinky swear that you will keep it

and I promise to share it with you.

Come with me as we skip through

the alligator swamp.

(Those are only my little brothers,

I promise they won't chomp.)

Step onto the stairs beneath you

and we will climb up the mountainside

that leads down the hall to the top-secret door.

It's a simple knock to get inside.

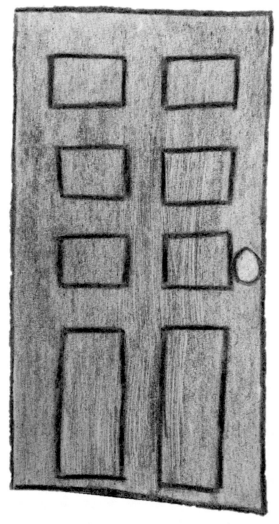

Welcome to the superheroes' kids secret club!

The place we all can feel accepted.

It's normal here for parents to deploy.

In fact, it is pretty much expected.

This secret isn't the biggest one though.

Are you ready to hear the news?

<u>Each one of us has a unique super kid power.</u>

Guess what? You have one too!

I'm serious! Just look at Aiden.
He has superhero kid speed.
He is the fastest one to notice
another kid in need.

Miguel is super smart.
He studies all kinds of bugs.

Anna is super caring.

She gives the greatest hugs.

Look out! Here comes Michael.

He is superhero kid strong.

He can lift up heavy boxes
and carry groceries for his mom.

Rebecca has super skills with words.
She helps us write all our letters.
She even reads to her younger sister
to make her feel a little better.

Ethan is a super-duper eater.
You should see him gobble lunch,

and MY super power is making friends.
I'm like the ambassador for our bunch.

Our only rule is to use our powers

always for only good.

Like our dads all asked us to.

Like all superheroes should.

Now here is your secret mission

as the newest member of our crew.

You must discover the super kid power

that is unique to you.

Then you use it to help others.

Well, at least you have to try.

Soon all the days your dad is away

will start to slip on by.

There are so many of us out there,

in every neighborhood and on every base.

We all have a special super kid power

and we all have a hard task to face.

So, we use our power and always remember

that none of us are in this alone.

The superheroes' kids and your family will be there

until your daddy comes back home.

Note from the illustrator

Hi everyone, my name is Angelica Rose Jacques. I am 16 years old and I was born in Okinawa, Japan. I am the proud daughter of a U.S. Marine. I have an older brother in college who is planning to enlist and a younger brother who one day wants to serve our country too. I am currently a junior in high school and concurrently enrolled in my local community college. I have been a military brat all my life. I know how hard deployments are and how they can seem a little scary. I am so happy to have the opportunity to illustrate this book for you all. I hope you enjoy my drawings.

About the Author

Heather Carson is a children's book author with a degree in Early Education. She is the wife of a U.S. Navy IDC and mother to a three-year-old boy with another baby on the way. She wrote this story on her husband's last deployment while helping their son cope with the separation.

Made in the USA
Middletown, DE
09 March 2019